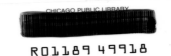

Separate Yet Sisters

Separate Yet Sisters

Susan Harkna

VANTAGE PRESS
New York

FIRST EDITION

Copyright © 1998 by Susan Harkna

Published by Vantage Press, Inc.
516 West 34th Street, New York, New York 10001

Manufactured in the United States of America
ISBN: 0-533-12358-5

Library of Congress Catalog Card No.: 97-90283

0 9 8 7 6 5 4 3 2 1

For Britt and Kristiana

Contents

Prologue   1

Part One: SARA
One   5
Two   11
Three   15
Four   19
Five   23
Six   27

Part Two: KATHLEEN
Seven   37
Eight   49
Nine   55

Part Three: ALEX
Ten   61
Eleven   67
Twelve   73
Thirteen   77

Epilogue   81

Separate Yet Sisters

Prologue

January was a particularly frigid month in Ellsworth, Iowa, in 1954. The sky was gray day after day with the threat of snow.

Jenny Nielson, however, was totally oblivious to the cold outside as she was sweating profusely inside giving birth to not one but three babies. Two babies had been expected, but the third tiny bundle had been hiding behind her sisters.

Jenny had screamed in pain and fear all during labor and part of the delivery but was now simply exhausted. She merely whimpered as the third child made its way into the world.

She was not even permitted to see her daughters before they were whisked away. All three were being adopted. Two had families waiting, but the third—a surprise—would have to be arranged for.

Jenny had been raised by her father after her mother died when Jenny was five. Her father was a good man with very strict morals. He thought he had passed these morals along to his only child but later realized he had failed miserably. Jenny became pregnant at sixteen.

Mr. Nielson made arrangements for Jenny to go live with his sister in Des Moines for the pregnancy and delivery. Families were found for the expected twins, and that was that.

After the births, Jenny was temporarily saddened over

returning home to Ellsworth without her babies, but soon settled back into life as a teenager. Her father switched her to another school, and she was forbidden to ever again see the offending boy who had fathered the babies.

Jenny was a very attractive young girl with waist-length blonde hair and sparkling green eyes. She soon enjoyed the attentions of other boys and quickly forgot the father of her three daughters.

In fact, she all but forgot about her babies. They crossed her mind from time to time, but she never knew who adopted them and never tried to find out. If she had, she would have known what was happening in each of their lives during their thirty-fifth year—in 1989.

Part One

SARA

Chapter One

They met quite by accident. Sara dearly loved her morning paper. Each day she got out of bed, opened all the blinds, went downstairs for a light breakfast, then briefly scanned the paper, which she finished on the train ride to work. This morning when she opened her door, there was no paper. Despite the cold January weather, she decided to dash out to the local drug store to get one. She threw on her wool coat over her nightgown and jumped into the car for the three-block trip. She parked and ran in, hoping no one would know she was in her nightgown. As she was backing out again, she collided with another car that was also backing out.

There she sat with no make-up on, hair uncombed and in her nightgown. She turned as there was a knock at her window. She found herself looking at a man with the most beautiful pair of blue eyes she had ever seen. She was momentarily stunned but quickly recovered and rolled down her window.

"I fear we've collided," the man said.

"I'm so sorry," Sara replied, "I'm afraid I wasn't looking. I was in a rush."

"My fault as well. I failed to look. Shall we pull over to an empty area and inspect the damage?"

Sara was mortified by her appearance but knew she had to look. She timidly got out of the car, wrapping the coat tightly around her. They bent over to look at the dented fenders.

"It's really not too bad," the man noticed. "Why don't we exchange names and insurance information and let them figure it out."

"If you're sure that's okay," Sara replied uncertainly. She never knew quite what to do in an accident.

"Yes, I'm quite sure."

They both wrote down the information and with apologies to each other once again, they were on their separate ways.

Sara swore to herself that she would never leave the house again in her nightgown. Her very next thought was what an interesting looking and sounding man he was. She detected a British accent, and he was such a gentleman. And those eyes—strikingly blue. She wished they had met under different circumstances. Since her divorce three years before, Sara hadn't had much interest in the opposite sex—until today. She shrugged and pulled into her parking space.

As her busy week went by, Sara all but forgot about the parking lot incident until her phone rang on a Thursday night. It was the man from the parking lot. He refreshed her memory, reminding her his name was Todd Knight. He had recently moved to the area from England, just as she had suspected.

"I've come here for two years to work on a special project. I live quite close to where we collided."

"I do too, just a few blocks away."

"Do you work in Northbrook as well?" Todd asked.

"No," Sara answered. "I work in downtown Chicago for a doctor.

"Are you a nurse?"

"No, I'm the office manager. What about you? Where do you work?"

"I'm doing special research at Abbott Laboratories in North Chicago," Todd replied.

"Oh, how interesting. Are you a scientist?"

"Yes, I work in genetic engineering. But why don't we discuss all of this at dinner? Would you like to have dinner with me tomorrow night?" Todd asked.

"Why, yes. I'd like that."

"Would you like to go to the Chelsea House right here in town?"

"Great—should I meet you there?" Sara asked.

"Okay, why don't we plan on 7:00 P.M."

"That's good, see you then," Sara replied, hanging up the phone with a smile on her face. There was just something about that man.

Sara felt like a school girl all the next day. She was so excited about the date that she kept watching the clock at work until finally she could leave. All the way home on the train, she planned what she would wear.

After changing clothes three times, Sara was out the door for the short drive to the restaurant. As she walked in, she felt nervous and wondered if Todd felt that way also. She looked much more polished than when they had met in the parking lot, but even then she was a natural beauty, with green eyes that tilted upward ever so slightly, small nose, lovely full, pink lips, and a wreath of heavenly blonde hair. She was slender and not very tall.

Sara was startled as Todd came up behind her.

"Oh, hi. I hope I didn't keep you waiting," she said.

"Not at all, you're just about on time."

They were shown to a table and Todd ordered a bottle of wine.

"Mmmm . . . this is good," Sara said as she took another swallow. "As much as I enjoy drinking it, I'm afraid my knowledge of wines is very limited. It's one of those areas that I want to explore but never quite get to."

"If it weren't for my father, I'd probably feel like you do.

He had a great interest in studying and sampling all types of wine, and involved my brother and me in it. He had a particular taste for German wines and made many trips through the Weintrasse in Germany visiting the vineyards."

"Did you get to go along?" Sara asked.

"Many times we did, but he died quite young—heart attack."

"Oh, I'm sorry. Is your mother still living?"

"Yes, she's back in England, living in London."

"Is your home also in London?" Sara asked.

"Yes and no. I have my own flat in London, but also a cottage in a small town about two hours outside of London called Burford. It's in the Cotswolds," Todd replied.

"Oh, I've been to London, but not to the countryside. It must be lovely."

"I think it is. I purchased the cottage two years ago, not knowing this research project would become available. I have my brother and his wife living there while I'm gone—which will be another year and a half."

As he spoke, Sara was again struck by the vivid blue of Todd's eyes. His black hair hung down a bit on his forehead, giving him a boyish look, but she estimated his age to be around thirty-eight. He also had a rugged build yet a gentle manner.

"Enough about me," Todd protested. "Let me hear about you. Have you always lived in Illinois?"

"No, I grew up in New Jersey and came to the Chicago area with my now ex-husband about seven years ago. I originally worked for a dentist but now have the office manager position for a Dr. Robbins. He's an internist."

"I'm sorry about your divorce. Was it rough?" Todd asked.

"It was pretty unpleasant, but at least no children were involved. Tom has gone back to New Jersey."

They took a minute out to order grilled salmon with dill sauce for Sara and sautéed veal with linguine for Todd.

After another sip of wine from the almost empty bottle, Sara asked, "And what about you? Have you ever been married?"

"No marriages, no children. I suppose I haven't found the right one yet."

"I'm sorry about the twenty questions, but can I ask one more?"

"Shoot."

"How about your research project at Abbott? I find that fascinating. Can you tell me a little about it?"

"Yes, but it's pretty technical. Briefly put, I'm working on genetic theories that predispose individuals to certain diseases. I'm lucky to have gotten the grant to conduct the research," Todd explained.

Their dinner arrived and for a while they were absorbed in enjoying it before resuming conversation and discovering they had a lot in common. Both liked photography, writing, movies, ethnic restaurants and especially, nature walks.

"Sara, you must try and plan on a trip to England, Scotland, and even Ireland. The walking in the countryside there is magnificent."

"I can imagine it is. I have three weeks vacation coming, and I'll consider that."

"Well," Todd said, "I suppose we should be going. I feel like I could talk with you for hours more, but work beckons us both tomorrow. How about a movie Saturday night?"

"I'd love it."

Chapter Two

Sara found herself falling in love. She had been seeing Todd almost every night for two months. Todd was so easy to be with and had a wonderful sense of humor—which surprised her coming from an Englishman. And he excited and stirred things deep inside of her.

"What would you think," Todd began as they relaxed comfortably in each others arms one evening, "of taking a weekend trip to Galena? I've never been there and hear it's beautiful."

"Oh, it is. It's incredible to find hills in Illinois, which is basically a very flat state. Apparently that's what makes it the tourist attraction that it is. It's in the northwest corner of the state, right near Iowa, so you can even see the Mississippi River. Too bad it's winter, though. In the fall, the leaves are dazzling. But if we get some snow, there will be a different kind of beauty."

They made reservations at a bed-and-breakfast, and made the three and a half hour trip in Todd's car the following weekend.

When they awoke their first morning and looked out the window, they were greeted by a winter wonderland. The snow-covered gently rolling hills all around them glistened in the bright sunshine.

"What a gift from nature. You must have connections," Todd marveled as he embraced Sara. "Let's go for a walk."

"I'll take you to my favorite look-out. It's quite a climb but it's worth it," Sara said.

Standing on the small, wooden platform at what felt like the top of the world, Todd took Sara gently into his arms and whispered, "Will you marry me? I know we've only known one another a short while, but I couldn't be more certain."

Sara knew Todd was right. This was their destiny: to be together. "Yes," she whispered back. And then louder, "Oh, yes!"

A small, private wedding was planned to take place in just three months. At thirty-five, Sara wasn't interested in a big event. After the wedding, Todd wanted to take his new bride honeymooning to his homeland.

"I'm anxious to show you my home in Burford and the splendors of Great Britain and Ireland," Todd said enthusiastically. "We have only three weeks, but since we're talking about moving to England once my grant is up, hopefully you can get an idea of what it's like."

"I feel that I'd most likely be happy anywhere as long as I was with you," Sara replied, kissing Todd softly on the lips.

Sara had friends in Chicago and liked her job, but she felt there was really nothing to keep her there. She could certainly find work, eventually, in England, and she could visit her parents periodically. She really did think the possibility of living abroad quite exhilarating.

*   *   *

May 31, alive with signs of spring, arrived and with four friends each in attendance, Todd and Sara were married. They had chosen to be married in a small chapel just outside of Northbrook, with the most spectacular stained-glass windows either had ever seen.

Sara's dress was made of soft, ivory silk chiffon with a

high neck and low back, which closed with many tiny mother-of-pearl buttons. It was knee length, which suited her small frame. Her blonde hair was swept up under a short veil. Her green eyes sparkled with excitement and emotion. She held a small bouquet of white-and-pink roses and baby's breath.

Todd, Sara thought, couldn't have looked more handsome. He was wearing a very dark suit and white dress shirt that complemented his black hair and unforgettable blue eyes. He seemed confident and not a bit nervous the way Sara remembered Tom had been at their wedding.

The only flaw was the absence of both Todd and Sara's parents, but they had decided to visit them instead on their way to the honeymoon destination and have parties in their honor.

At the conclusion of the ceremony, Todd looked down at Sara, tilted her chin upwards, and kissed her, saying, "I do love you, Mrs. Knight. We'll have a great life and grow old and gray together."

Sara felt as if she would simply burst with love for this man.

Chapter Three

On the flight to visit Sara's parents in New Jersey, on their way to England, Todd turned to Sara.

"Your mother and dad sound so very nice on the phone, but what do you really suppose they'll think of me?"

"Hmm . . . let's see. I'm sure they will think you a mysterious, dangerous foreigner or a boring Englishman," said Sara.

Todd tickled her. "No, really."

"Okay, okay. They'll love you, how could they not?"

"I guess I'll just have to wait and see for myself," Todd said.

Sara's father met them at the Newark Airport. Sara could see his anxious eyes scanning the passengers as they approached the baggage area. At sixty-five, he was still a nice-looking man: tall, silver haired, and trim. She knew her mother would be waiting at home. Her arthritis had become so bad over the past two years that she was now in a wheelchair.

"Heh, Dad!" Sara signaled.

Their eyes met and each face spread into a wide grin.

"You're right on time," her father said as he embraced his only child.

"Dad, this is Todd. Todd, this is my dad."

"Glad to meet you, sir," Todd said, shaking hands.

"Oh, call me Jim, please. Good to meet you as well. Let's get the bags. Mother is so excited to see you two."

It was a short drive to Hillside.

Sara was anxious to see her mom as she hadn't done so in almost a year. She felt badly about this, but the time never seemed right to fly out. It was going to break her heart to see her mom in a wheelchair.

Pulling up, Sara saw her mother's expectant face in the window. Upon seeing the car, that face became wreathed in smiles.

"I've brought them, Mother," Jim called out as they entered the house.

Sara ran to her mother and leaned down to give her a huge hug and kiss. "I've missed you, Mom. How are you feeling?"

"Don't worry about me. I'm just fine. Your dad gets good exercise pushing me around. I've missed you too, Sara, but thank goodness we talk on the phone often. Now, who do we have here?" Sara's mother asked, turning to Todd.

"So good to meet you, Mrs. Kenson."

"Please call me Mom or Barbara, dear. It's just wonderful to meet you."

Sara wasn't as upset as she thought she would be at seeing her mother in the wheelchair. She was still lovely with her long, mostly gray hair pulled back in a neat bun. And the mischievous merriment could still be seen in her dark brown eyes. She seemed small in the big chair, but then she had always been petite.

They enjoyed a casual dinner that evening, and Barbara explained that the party to introduce the new bride and groom would be the following evening.

"We've invited about forty friends and relatives," Barbara said excitedly. "We're having it catered and served, so you don't have to worry about my wearing myself out, Sara."

"Good," said Sara. "That was a concern I had. We'll have

16

to go over the list later so Todd can acquaint himself with our humorous family."

"Well, if they're that humorous that they need a pre-introduction, I will truly look forward to meeting them in the flesh," Todd said, laughing.

The next day Sara showed Todd around Hillside. After she showed him the downtown area, her high school, and favorite park, they stopped for coffee.

"I'm really enjoying this, Sara," Todd said. "Seeing your roots helps me to know you even better."

"Well, I'm not going to tell you all my deepest, darkest secrets," Sara said teasingly as she kissed him.

*   *   *

The party was a success. Todd seemed to enjoy being introduced to everyone. Sara could see that he especially liked her Uncle Nick, who had endless tales to tell.

Her best friend from childhood was also there. Her nickname was Tooty, but her real name was Diana. Tooty had stayed in Hillside after marrying her high school sweetheart, Jamie. It was good to see Tooty again, Sara thought, even though she was flirting with Todd. Tooty hadn't changed much. She still had her long, almost kinky black hair. She had gained some weight, but it suited her as she had been extremely skinny growing up. She and Jamie had three children. Jamie was a partner now in his father's hardware store, and Tooty stayed home with the children. They appeared happy, but Sara hadn't talked with Tooty in a long time.

"Boy, Sara, Todd is a honey," Tooty whispered when they had a moment together. "I just love his accent. Your mother said you met him in Chicago. Does he have any brothers? No, only kidding. I love good old Jamie, but it's been a long time since I've had any excitement."

"Everyone knew you two would always be together, Toot, excitement or no excitement. And you're so lucky to have three kids. Tom and I never got it together enough to start a family," Sara replied. "But Todd and I plan to down the road."

"Well, don't wait too long, they're exhausting."

Sara stood back and observed Todd. He was charming, and she was so proud of him as he moved around the room chatting easily.

Later that night when they were alone again, Todd said, "You know, I quite like your family and friends, and I think they approve of me. What do you think?"

"I already told you they'd adore you. But I get to adore you the very most."

Todd kissed the tip of Sara's nose. "Are you ready for the next leg of our trip? I'm anxious for you to meet Mother. And don't ask me if she'll like you, because I already know she will."

Chapter Four

Two days later Todd and Sara were taxiing down the runway on British Airways flight 828 to London. It was a night flight, and they slept fitfully some of the way, arriving London time 7:00 A.M.

"We'll get a taxi to Mother's house in Knightsbridge for a quick hello, then go on to my flat for some sleep," Todd said, steering a sleepy Sara through the crowds.

"That sounds perfect. I could use some quality zzzs with my hubby right about now."

Sara felt a bit anxious about meeting Todd's mother. She had sounded quite reserved on the phone the several times they had talked.

The taxi dropped them off in front of an elegant brown-and-white townhome with a black wrought-iron gate. Todd explained that he had grown up here, but preferred to have his own flat. His father had left his mother financially secure when he died, so she was able to stay in her home.

Todd rang the bell, and they were met at the door by a tall woman with stylishly short salt-and-pepper colored hair. She was smartly dressed in a white silk blouse and tweed skirt. And after seeing her beautiful blue eyes, Sara knew this was Todd's mother.

"Hello, Son," Todd's mother said as she embraced Todd. "Six months has been too long."

"It's good to see you also. Mother, this is Sara, my beautiful new bride."

"I can see why you waited so long to marry. She is lovely, dear. Very nice to meet you, Sara," Mrs. Knight said in a cool yet not unfriendly way.

"And it's very nice to meet you. I've been looking forward to this, Mrs. Knight," Sara replied, as she extended her hand.

"You may call me 'Mother' if you'd like. Mrs. Knight sounds a bit too stuffy even for me. Well, I'm sure you're both tired and hungry after a night flight. I've had Matty put out some tea, croissants, and ham and cheese for you."

Sara found she was hungry and ate with relish but was relieved when Todd said they would be going onto his flat now for a nap.

"Ring me up later, and I'll give you the details of the dinner I have planned for you both tomorrow evening," Mrs. Knight said, as she opened the door for them.

Todd and Sara took a taxi to Todd's flat in Kensington.

"It's been so long since I've been to London. I'd love for you to show me around tomorrow," Sara said.

"It will be my pleasure. Here we are now," Todd said, as the taxi stopped in front of another townhome—all white with brown trim and larger than Mrs. Knight's.

As they approached the front door, Sara saw six bells and mailboxes. "You have quite a few neighbors, I see."

"Only five. I don't see much of them," Todd replied, as he unexpectedly scooped Sara up in his arms. "Do let me carry you over the threshold, Mrs. Knight."

Sara giggled. "Who knew you were such a romantic, Mr. Knight?"

The flat was small but adequate. The combination living/dining room was decorated in sleek modern designs of black and white. There was a small kitchen and one bedroom.

"Let's stop right here," Todd said when Sara peered into the bedroom. Arms intertwined they tumbled onto the bed

20

in a sudden surge of passion—all thoughts of sleep temporarily pushed aside.

The next morning Todd showed Sara around London as promised. It was a beautiful spring day—warm with a gentle breeze. The trees and flowers were blooming in the ritual of life renewed. She saw his favorite pub, the hospital where his lab was, homes of some friends and the prestigious Eaton Academy that he attended before going to Oxford University.

They stopped for lunch at a restaurant on High Street in Kensington.

"I find London fascinating," Sara said. "It must have been fabulous growing up here—so much to do."

"I guess I took it for granted, but you're right, there are many opportunities here. Now let's drive through Covent Garden, and I'll show you the restaurant Mother has chosen for our dinner tonight."

Todd drove the car past Buckingham Palace, Trafalgar Square, and on into Covent Garden.

"Did you know that Trafalgar Square is the very center of London?" Todd asked Sara.

"Actually, I do remember that, but I've forgotten the significance of Covent Garden."

"Well, the Royal Opera House is here, plus it's a major shopping, restaurant, and café district. There's 'Rules' now. It's the oldest and most celebrated restaurant in London—built in 1798."

"Wow, your mother does things right. I can't wait to see the inside tonight."

They returned early afternoon to Todd's flat to rest a bit before dinner. Sara felt nervous about meeting Todd's friends and family, but he'd had to do the same thing at her home and survived the ordeal.

On the way to pick up Mrs. Knight, Todd took hold of

Sara's hand. "Don't look so worried. You'll like them. They're mostly my friends, not Mother's."

Sara showed him a wan smile. "Oh, I'll be fine. I'll only be in a room with twenty-five complete strangers—foreign strangers at that."

As they entered the restaurant, Sara felt as if she had stepped back in time. They climbed a narrow, winding staircase to the Edwardian dining room, a private dining room on the second floor. The entire room was red velvet with signed portraits of English kings, Charles Dickens, John Barrymore, Clark Gable, and Sir Lawrence Olivier adorning the walls.

Immediately they were surrounded by Todd's friends and family. There was much back-slapping, hand-shaking, and hugs all around. "But where is your brother, Nigel, and his wife?" Sara asked as she managed a few words with Todd.

"I just found out that they couldn't make it, but we'll see them tomorrow when we drive to Burford. By the way, I love you, darling. Having a good time?"

"It's a bit confusing, but yes."

They eventually sat down and Sara was seated at the head of the table with Todd. To her right was Todd's favorite cousin, Henry, and across from Henry was his wife, Vanessa. They proved to be very entertaining with numerous stories of Todd and Henry's escapades while growing up.

Sara was overwhelmed by the menu. There were angels on horseback (oysters wrapped in bacon and served on toast), Aylebury duckling, wild Scottish salmon, partridge, and roast rib of Scottish beef to name a few. She chose roast beef with Yorkshire pudding, roasted new potatoes with onion, and English goat cheese salad with garlic dressing.

There was an enormous cake for dessert and champagne toasts were offered all around for the new bride and groom.

Chapter Five

"I love, love, love you, Mrs. Knight," Todd whispered into Sara's ear as they lay in each other's arms in Todd's flat after the party. "Now that we've gotten all the family obligations behind us, are you ready to head into the country?" Todd asked.

"I sure am. Why don't we leave first thing when we wake up tomorrow?"

They packed up and got into Todd's navy blue Alpha Romeo by 2:00 P.M. Sara was extremely excited to see Burford and Todd's cottage as they might one day soon be her new home. The trip was expected to take just about two hours.

After leaving London, the scenery turned pastoral. Sara was enchanted by the lushly green fields and quaint homes along the way. Todd took her past his alma mater, Oxford University, then on into the Cotswolds.

"What exactly are the Cotswolds?" Sara asked.

"The Cotswolds are actually an area of limestone hills covered with grass and barren plateaus known as wolds. Cotswold lambs made the area very rich, and the architecture made out of Cotswold stone is some of the finest in Europe."

"So it's really named after the plateaus or wolds," Sara replied delighted by what she saw around her.

"Right. There's a Cotswold stone house over there. See the thatched roof? They last for about twenty-five years with periodic repairs."

"How fascinating. Does your house have a thatched roof?"

"I think I'll make you wait and see," Todd replied in a teasing tone.

They continued through ancient villages and hamlets until reaching Burford. Todd's cottage was just outside of downtown Burford. He pulled the car up next to a quaint stone house with, to Sara's delight, a thatched roof. It had a magnificent array of red, white, pink, yellow, and purple flowers everywhere she looked. They were in windowsill planters, pots on the ground and in the large garden adjacent to the southside of the house.

"Oh, Todd, it's charming. No wonder you fell in love with it," Sara said.

The front door opened and Todd's brother, Nigel, and Nigel's wife, Sydney, came out to greet them. Nigel was very tall and thin, with an immense, bushy, black mustache. Sydney was also tall, with the shortest hairstyle Sara had ever seen on a woman.

"Welcome, we've missed you these past months, Todd," Nigel said, as he embraced his brother warmly. "And so good to meet you, Sara."

"Yes, we are indeed," Sydney chimed in.

"And I'm happy to meet both of you," Sara replied, shaking hands.

"So sorry we missed the party last night, but it couldn't be helped," Nigel said.

"It's okay, old man. We knew we'd be seeing you today," Todd replied.

"Come on in. Let's give Sara the tour," Sydney said.

Entering the house, Sara was amazed by the difference between Todd's flat in London and this cottage. This was old-world charm, with beautiful antiques in each room compared to the modern decor of the flat. She liked them both, but couldn't immediately decide which she preferred.

"These antiques are lovely, Todd. Whenever did you have time to collect them?" Sara asked.

"I've been acquiring them for some time and stored them at Mother's. Nigel has also been looking for me. I'm anxious to see the three new pieces you sent me the photos of, Nige."

Sydney's voice rang out, calling them to dinner. They ate with relish the roasted rack of lamb, with creamy garlic potatoes and carrots.

"This is simply delicious, Sydney," Sara said. "I can tell you enjoy cooking."

"I do. Since we moved here from Stratford to house-sit for Todd, I'm enjoying the life of leisure. I look after the house and flowers and practice my culinary skills on Nigel here. I worked as a secretary in Stratford and took a leave to come here."

"What about you, Nigel?" Sara asked. "Todd says you are a dentist. Are you practicing here or are you also on leave?"

"No, I'm working here in Burford with another dentist. It seems he has a heavy patient load and welcomes the help."

Listening to the talk, Sara felt good. If everyone in Burford was as friendly as Nigel and Sydney, Sara thought she could make the transition of moving here quite easily.

"Hey, Todd," Nigel said, "why don't you map out the rest of your trip with this lovely lady for us?"

"I haven't even gone over it with Sara yet to see if she approves, but if it's okay with her, I'll give you all an overview."

"Please, I'm anxious to hear where my tour guide is taking me," Sara replied, smiling.

Todd spread out the map. "Well, first I'd like to drive

the short way up to Stratford to show you where Nigel and Sydney live and the birthplace of William Shakespeare. From there to Lincoln to show you the eleventh century Lincoln Cathedral. It has the second highest tower in England. Then we'll go to York where we'll stay at the Bilbrough Manor. It's charming, plus has great food."

"We've eaten there," interjected Sydney. "The food really is divine."

"After York, we'll head for the Yorkshire Dales National Park for a few days of hiking. I think you'll like it, Sara. It's all water-carved—interesting shapes and formations."

"Taking her to Hadrian's Wall after that?" Nigel asked.

"Definitely—to Hexam and Hadrian's Wall. The wall, Sara, was built in A.D. 122 and stretches seventy-three miles from the North Sea to the Irish Sea. See, it's right here on the map. There are some spectacular views from the wall."

"I can't wait to see it all. Good thing I have lots of film," Sara said.

"Then we're almost to Scotland. Would you like to visit Glasgow and Edinburgh, Sara?" Todd asked.

"I would, plus some smaller villages like we've seen here in England."

"Sounds like a good trip. Wish we could go with you, especially to Scotland. We've not been there in a long time, have we, Sydney?" Nigel asked.

"No, but we can go sometime when you have a break, my love."

"She takes good care of me, that Sydney," Nigel said, smiling and giving his wife a hug.

Chapter Six

"What a beautiful day for a trip," Todd remarked as he and Sara packed up the car. It was a beauty—warm with a cloudless blue sky and a gentle spring sun.

After saying their good-byes, the new Mr. and Mrs. Knight set off.

"I thoroughly enjoyed myself here, Todd. Not only are Nigel and Sydney the best, but everyone you introduced me to in Burford is so friendly."

"I know it's early yet, but do you have any idea as to whether you might like to live here? In London or Burford, or both?"

"I adore London, but have been charmed by Burford. I think both!" Sara replied enthusiastically.

"We could pick out another flat in London, if you'd like, and decorate it together. But do you think you'd be happy in the cottage on weekends and holidays?" Todd asked, a bit anxiously. "Is Burford too far in the country for you?"

Sara leaned over and kissed Todd. She studied him a bit before answering. She felt so much love for him. He was capable, yet gentle and good. His hair had grown longer, making him look more boyish and appealing than ever.

"Todd, I would live anywhere with you. You have taught me how to love again and have brought so much joy into my life. But to answer your question, it might be fun to find our own flat in London. The cottage, on the other hand, stays just as it is. I love it and Burford."

"And I love you. Thank you, Sara."

They drove the forty minutes to Stratford engaged in amiable conversation. Sara was surprised to see how big Stratford was. It had grown into quite the tourist spot as the result of Will Shakespeare. Todd took Sara past Shakespeare's birthplace, past Nigel and Sydney's lovely stone home, and to the Avon River with its brightly colored tourist boats. They stopped for lunch at a small café that offered sandwiches and soup.

"Next stop, Lincoln," Todd said as they climbed back into the car for the two-hour ride.

Sara thoroughly enjoyed watching the scenery fly by as they drove past quaint villages and fields with lambs grazing. The day was bright and their spirits matched it when Todd suddenly clutched his chest.

"Sara," he barely whispered, "pain. . . ." He slumped over the steering wheel, and Sara wildly maneuvered the car to the side of the road.

No, she thought, then aloud, "No, this is not happening. You are just fine, Todd. You're kidding, aren't you? You're joking, but it's not funny!"

He looked so lifeless. Panic grabbed Sara and she shouted while mindlessly shaking him, "Wake up. Oh, please, wake up." And in a quiet whisper with tears streaming down her face, "I've only just begun to love you."

Terror engulfed Sara and made her take action. She knew she had to get help. She saw a house not too far away. She ran, arriving wild-eyed and screaming. The man inside calmed her enough to find out her husband was unconscious in their car just down the road. He guided Sara into his car, and they drove the short distance to the Alpha Romeo.

Todd had not moved. The man quickly opened the car door and felt Todd's neck for a pulse.

"I'm afraid," the man said softly and gently as he turned towards Sara, "there is no pulse."

Of course, Sara thought wildly. Why hadn't she checked and started CPR immediately? She had panicked and could think of nothing else but getting help.

Trembling all over, Sara collected herself enough to take action. "Please help me get him into the back of your car and then to the nearest hospital. I think he's had a heart attack."

"I'm sorry, ma'am, there is only the doctor's office. I'll take you there right away."

As soon as Todd was in the back seat, Sara started the CPR she knew but had never had to use before. She was steady now, willing Todd's heart to start again with each breath and each compression of his chest that she administered.

Ten minutes later Todd was on the examining table at the doctor's office. Only then did Sara dissolve once again in tears. "Oh, please," she heard herself crying, "you have to save him."

The young doctor and his nurse worked over Todd's still body for what seemed like an eternity to Sara. When the doctor finally turned to Sara, she knew Todd was gone—had been gone since he slumped over the steering wheel.

"I'm sorry," the doctor began, looking sadly into Sara's red rimmed eyes. "There just wasn't anything we could do for your husband. If only we could have gotten him to hospital immediately after he suffered the attack."

Sara turned away. Just as Todd's heart had stopped beating, her heart had turned to stone. She felt as if she'd plunged into a deep, dark hole.

*   *   *

Todd's body was transported to London where an

autopsy revealed he had indeed suffered a massive heart attack.

They buried him in a small cemetery next to his beloved cottage in Burford.

Sara, Todd's mother, Nigel, and Sydney clung to one another in their shared grief, but Sara felt little comfort. She wished she had died also. Todd had become her life, her reason for being.

"Sara, why don't you stay here in England with us until you decide what you want to do?" Sydney suggested kindly.

"No, I think I'll go back to Chicago. I've got my job there, my apartment. Everything here reminds me too much of Todd. It's too painful."

Sara flew back to Chicago—to her job, her apartment, her friends—but it seemed an endless, empty life ahead of her.

*   *   *

Early summer was in bloom gloriously once again. All the trees were clothed in bright, fresh green leaves. Flowers were providing a riot of colors for all to see. This had always been Sara's favorite season, but not this year. It only made her feel more sad, more empty.

Sara entered back into the routine of her life, but with little enthusiasm. She contemplated moving to downtown Chicago to escape memories of Todd all around her in Northbrook, but realized wherever she went, she would never get him out of her heart.

"I love you, Todd," she sighed aloud. "How do I go on without you?"

In addition to her depression and grieving, Sara started to feel ill physically—probably making herself sick, she thought. She mentioned this to her co-worker, Mary.

"Why don't you talk to Dr. Robbins about it, Sara? You know how understanding he is," suggested Mary.

Sara decided to do just that. At the end of the day, she knocked on Dr. Robbins's office door. He was a kind man, looking older than his sixty years, with pure white hair and a slight stoop to his shoulders.

"Come in, Sara."

"I just wanted to thank you for being so patient with me, Dr. Robbins. I just can't seem to come to terms with my grief, and now I'm feeling nauseous much of the time. Do you think I should consider counseling?"

"Well, Sara, counseling is always helpful, but I also feel a thorough physical exam is in order. Why not start with your gynecologist?"

"Excuse me," Sara replied, "my gynecologist?"

"Yep, sounds to me as if you may be pregnant. Have you missed your period?"

"Pregnant? I never even thought of that. I've been in such a stupor lately. I have missed a period but attributed that to stress and grief," said a dazed Sara.

"Well, I suggest you give your gynecologist a call."

"I will," Sara said as she walked out of Dr. Robbins's office with the possibility of being pregnant sinking in. Could it be? Could she have a part of Todd living on inside of her?

*   *   *

Sara walked into Dr. Wagner's sixth-floor office with butterflies in her stomach, but she was feeling more hopeful about things than she had been since the tragedy.

Several women sat waiting, one with a small child. Sara had always known she wanted children one day and that she was getting older, but when she and Todd had talked about it, they had decided to wait for a year or two to start a family. She thought they had taken precautions.

"Sara," the nurse beckoned from the inner office, "come on in."

"Yes, coming," Sara said, rising on wobbly legs. She found herself hoping more by the minute that she was pregnant.

Sara was shown into a treatment room, and Dr. Wagner came in. The sight of him never failed to bring a smile to her face. He was a middle-aged man who wore his brown hair in a crew cut and favored glasses with red frames.

"How are you, Sara? I haven't seen you in about a year. Here for a check-up?"

"Hi, Dr. Wagner. Actually I'm here for a pregnancy test. I was remarried since you last saw me."

"How nice for you. And who is the lucky fellow?"

Sara lowered her eyes. She still had trouble talking about Todd's death. "He died—on our honeymoon."

"Oh, I'm so sorry, Sara. What a shock for you," Dr. Wagner said, putting a hand on her shoulder in sympathy.

"I haven't handled it too well. I've also felt ill lately and missed a period."

"Would it be a good thing if you are pregnant?"

"Right now, it would be the best news you could give me."

"Well, let's find out then," Dr. Wagner said.

After examining Sara, Dr. Wagner looked up with a twinkle in his eye. "Congratulations, you are indeed pregnant—about eight weeks."

Sara let out the breath she felt she'd been holding for a very long time. It was replaced with a smile she could not suppress from that moment on. She felt alive once more. She would never again feel Todd's tender touch or have his unwavering love to sustain her, but nonetheless she had a joyous reason to go on living.

Part Two

KATHLEEN

Chapter Seven

Kathleen stopped her nimble fingers from flying across the keyboard. She looked up from her computer and stared at the large, yellow, stone house across the alley. As always, an uneasy feeling passed through her. She then turned her gaze to her bedroom, which doubled as an office. Since her divorce two years ago, Kathleen had redecorated it. John had insisted on stripes and geometric shapes in hues of brown and gold. It was now festooned in Kathleen's favorites of yellow and navy, with flowers, ruffles, and plump, soft cushions everywhere. At just five feet tall, Kathleen was very pretty with shoulder-length blonde hair. Her most striking feature was her bright green eyes. To look at her you would say her bedroom suited her quite well.

She snapped out of her musings to continue with the task at hand. She had an article to finish that was due on her editor's desk tomorrow. She had worked for *Health Today* ever since the divorce had ended her eleven-year marriage. She enjoyed the job, having always been interested in health issues.

Kathleen's thoughts drifted once again as she thought of her girls, Jamie and Melissa. The divorce had been hard on both girls, but the post-divorce amicable relationship with their father helped a lot. Jamie, who was now ten, looked like John—with dark hair and eyes. She was on the serious side and very, very kind. Melissa, having just turned thirteen, was boisterous, enthusiastic, and every bit a teenager. She had her father's dark eyes but her mother's blonde hair. Kathleen loved them both so very much.

Kathleen worked for another hour. A soft, floral scented breeze reached out and touched her on the cheek. She loved the spring when she could open all the windows as wide as they would go. The roar of an engine and squeal of tires broke the peaceful calm of the lovely day. Kathleen knew at once that it was their neighbor, Billy, racing his car up and down the alley that separated their houses.

In their town of Merion, an upper class suburb of Philadelphia, Billy was an oddity with his albino looks. An oddity at the least and a threat to all at the most. Of the six kids who had grown up in the yellow house directly across the alley from Kathleen's, Billy was the only bad apple. And he was the reason that she felt uneasy whenever she looked over there. He had spent at least half of his twenty-eight years in jail, in rehab, dead drunk, or high on drugs. There were even rumors that he was involved in organized crime in Philadelphia. He came and went from his parents' home across the alley, and no one was ever quite sure how long he would stay.

Kathleen and her girls were wary and even frightened of him—he had such a strange, evil look in his eyes. When he was home, he seemed to take great pleasure in racing his old gray Chevy, which he stored in his parents' backyard, up and down the alley as he was doing now. His license had been revoked years ago, so this was the extent of his driving.

Kathleen hated what Billy made her confront about herself—her fear. She was afraid of Billy. She didn't like to admit she was afraid of anything, but knew down deep she was. And she was reminded of it each time she looked across the alley.

Suddenly, Kathleen felt enraged by Billy's noisy tire squeals and ran down the stairs and dashed to the back door.

She momentarily shed her fear and was going to tell him exactly what she thought of this exhibition. As she opened the door, her nightmare began. She was just in time to see Billy run into a young girl on her bike.

Terror for the child engulfed Kathleen. She ran out as Billy pulled his car into his backyard. She looked down at the child, who was unconscious, maybe dead. There was a large amount of blood surrounding her head, staining the black pavement. So much blood. Kathleen stared in horror. In an instant, Billy had her arm.

"That dumb kid, she got in my way," he snarled. "If you tell anyone, I'll kill your daughters."

Kathleen felt faint, but she had to keep control of herself. She had to get help for the little girl. She struggled out of his grip and ran into her house to call 911. She was trembling all over, knees very weak. She fumbled with the phone and finally got through to the 911 operator. She explained what had happened—that a young girl had been hit by a car while riding her bike, and the location. She then went out to sit with the girl until the paramedics arrived. The child still did not stir, she looked lifeless. Why wasn't she wearing a helmet? She looked to be about ten. Why hadn't her parents insisted on a helmet?

Kathleen was overcome with grief for the little girl, the poor, sweet innocent, so like her Jamie. She started to sob as the sirens could be heard close by. As the emergency vehicle drew up to them, the paramedics jumped out and began to work on the child. Soon the police were there also, asking Kathleen questions. What had she seen? Who had hit the girl? Could she give them a description? Kathleen remembered Billy's threat and was too frightened to tell the truth. So she told them that it was a hit-and-run, a dark blue car was driving off when she came outside. She couldn't see the driver or remember the license plates.

The little girl was alive, but just barely. The paramedics carefully placed her into the ambulance and sped off. The police loaded her bike into their patrol car.

The only thing left was the blood on the street.

Kathleen looked across the alley at the yellow house. Billy was staring at her from the kitchen window. A dark, threatening stare. She shivered and went inside.

She sat down with a brandy to calm herself. What if the child died? She would be an accomplice to murder. Was it murder? She had to tell someone, had to get advice. But whom could she tell? She knew she had to tell the police but didn't trust the judicial system. How long would it be before Billy was released and carried out his threat?

Just then Kathleen heard Jamie come in the back door, eyes wide. "Mommy, there's something strange in the alley. What is it?"

"It's blood, Jamie. I'm afraid a young girl riding her bike was hit by a car," Kathleen said softly, trying not to frighten her child.

"It's scary—all that blood," Jamie said.

"I know, honey, it is scary. Why don't you run upstairs to your room, and I'll come up in a minute and we'll talk about it."

"Okay, Mommy."

Kathleen started to pace. She kept going over and over what Billy had said. What should she do? Whom could she tell? Once she told one person, everyone else would find out. She couldn't take the chance and risk the lives of her children. Her dear, sweet, beautiful daughters with their whole lives ahead of them.

She looked out the kitchen window and saw Billy washing his car—trying to get rid of evidence, she assumed. He didn't seem hurried or guilty or upset in any way.

Kathleen's older daughter, Melissa, also arrived home—with questions.

"What's up in the alley?" she asked. "It looks like blood."

"It's serious," Kathleen replied. "A young girl was hit by a car, and I don't know if she is alive or dead. I called an ambulance right after it happened. I'm going to call the hospital soon to hear if they know anything about her condition."

"Wow, who hit her? Was she just walking down the alley?"

"She was on her bike, and no, I didn't see who hit her, just a blue car drive away. I'm so upset, the poor little girl."

"I can see you're upset. Do you know who she is?" Melissa asked.

"I have no idea. I guess when she doesn't go home, her parents will call the police and they'll find her. Jamie is upset. Please go up and talk to her. I'll be up in a minute."

Kathleen sat there thinking. She had to tell someone, she needed advice. She would scream if she couldn't. She dialed her ex-husband's number, but he was in a meeting. She tried her boyfriend, Jake, but he was out. Her last hope was her best friend, Maureen. Her fingers shook as she dialed the number. Two, three rings, then yes, there was the familiar voice.

"Good afternoon, Mr. Thompson's office. This is Maureen speaking."

"Maureen, this is Kathleen. A terrible thing has happened, can you talk?"

"Let me ask Sally to take my calls, and I'll switch phones," Maureen replied, anxiously. "There, I'm back. What happened?"

"I was working on the computer when I heard my neighbor, Billy, racing his car in the alley. I went outside to

41

ask him to stop but instead saw him hit a young girl on her bike."

"Oh, my God, Kathleen. How terrible. Is she okay? Did she need an ambulance?"

"She was unconscious when the ambulance took her to the hospital. She looked very bad."

"What about Billy?" Maureen asked. "Did the police arrest him?"

"That's the problem—my problem. When I raced outside, Billy grabbed my arm and said if I told the police he was responsible, he would kill my girls. You know how evil he is. I believe him. I don't know what to do, I'm so upset and afraid."

"If you tell the police, they'll arrest him and put him in jail, so he couldn't harm you or the girls," Maureen offered.

"But he's been in jail many times and always released in a short while."

After a pause, Kathleen said, "I have to tell the police, don't I?"

"Just think if it were your child. Wouldn't you want to know who was responsible?"

"You're right, okay. I'll call them," Kathleen replied reluctantly. Maureen had been Kathleen's best friend for twenty years, and Kathleen always relied upon her good judgment.

"Good luck," Maureen said.

Kathleen was shaking again as she dialed the local police department. "I want to report a hit-and-run accident that I witnessed," she told the answering voice.

"Give me your name and address, and I'll send a detective over to get your statement," the voice said briskly.

"I'm Kathleen VanDuran at 86 Greenbriar Lane."

"Okay, we'll send a detective right away."

Kathleen waited nervously, pacing up and down the

beautiful wood floors she had polished only yesterday. The detective arrived in ten minutes. She opened the door to a middle-aged man with the brightest red hair she had ever seen.

"Hello, I'm Detective Sullivan. I understand you witnessed a hit-and-run accident," he said in a gentle way.

"Yes," Kathleen replied anxiously. "It was this morning in the alley by my house. A young girl on her bike was hit by my neighbor in his car. The police were there, but I didn't tell them because he said he'd kill my girls if I did. He's been in trouble with the police before and they never seem to detain him long. I'm truly afraid for my family. This man is extremely dangerous."

"And what is your neighbor's name and address?" the detective asked.

"His name is Billy Wilson, and he lives at times directly across the alley from me at 84 Hilldale."

"Well, I'm glad you came forward because I know about this case. The young girl unfortunately died from her injuries," the detective said, looking pained.

Kathleen gasped and shook her head. "I'm so sorry, that poor child. Her family must be devastated."

"It's a tragedy, and they are very anxious for this information. Don't worry about Mr. Wilson. We'll investigate and have him in custody tonight."

"If for any reason," Kathleen pleaded, "you don't arrest him, please tell me. Believe me when I say he is capable of carrying out his threats. Actually, please let me know when he has been arrested."

"We'll let you know," the detective said as he closed the door. "And try not to worry."

Kathleen knew she now had to tell her daughters. She called them down to the kitchen.

"It's about the accident today," she began. "It was our

neighbor Billy who ran over the girl. I saw it. The reason I didn't tell you was that I didn't want to frighten you. Billy threatened to harm us if I told the police he did it. Also, the little girl died."

Both girls looked shocked and frightened.

"Did you tell the police, Mom?" Melissa asked.

"Yes, I just gave my report to a detective."

"Will they arrest him right away?" an anxious Jamie asked.

"The detective said they'd investigate immediately."

"Do you think Billy will come after us since you turned him in?" Melissa asked.

"Well, if he's in jail, how can he hurt us?" Kathleen answered.

"Will there be a trial? Will you have to testify?" Melissa asked.

"I don't know anything more than what I told you. We'll have to wait to hear from the police. To be safe until we do hear, let's just stay in the house."

Kathleen kept looking over at the yellow house and could see no sign of Billy.

In no time at all, two black-and-white squad cars came into the alley and parked by Billy's house. One officer went to the door and another two checked his car and tire tracks. Billy left his car in the backyard with only dirt and grass as a driveway.

As she watched, Kathleen saw the officer go into the house. Ten minutes later he came out with Billy in handcuffs. At seeing Billy, Kathleen started to tremble. What had she done? She knew she had to turn him in, but would she and the girls ever be safe again?

"Mom," Melissa shouted as she ran down the stairs, "the police are taking Billy away."

"I know, I see. Now we just have to wait to hear if they are holding him."

They continued to look out the window. The one squad car left with Billy. He was slumped down in the back seat—white hair barely visible. The other two officers stayed to photograph the car and take samples.

There was no sign of any of the other family members. The house looked eerily quiet. Kathleen felt sorry for Pat and Hank, Billy's parents. They were quiet, meek people who kept to themselves. Pat, with deep lines in her pale face, looked old before her time—no doubt due to her youngest son. Kathleen knew that Billy was not on good terms with his family, so she doubted they would pay his bail, if it was even set. She hoped they wouldn't. What would she do if somehow he did get out on bail?

Kathleen felt drained yet agitated. She wanted to talk to Jake. Like Maureen, he had a calming effect on her. She put in another call to him, and this time he was there.

"Oh, Jake, I'm so glad you're there. You won't believe what happened."

"Calm down, Kathleen, and tell me."

"This morning our neighbor, Billy, ran over a girl on her bike with his car and killed her. I witnessed the entire thing, and he threatened to kill my girls if I told the police."

"You must tell the police," Jake replied immediately.

"I did, I did. A Detective Sullivan came and took my statement a little while ago. Then several patrol cars arrived at Billy's house, and they took him away. I'm really frightened."

"Don't worry. I doubt they'll allow bail for him since he has a long criminal record, and I'm sure they have evidence taken from his car. I'll come over tonight and we can talk more," Jake said.

"Okay—please come as soon as you can."

Oh, Jake, thought Kathleen after hanging up, *I do love you so.* This man, not only strong in stature, but also in character. Kathleen had fallen in love with him almost immediately. They met a year ago at a wine-tasting. Something about the lopsided grin, kind look in his eyes, and perfect manners endeared him to her. He even liked the girls, and his being thirty-two to her thirty-five years did not bother her at all.

Jake arrived early. Kathleen was so relieved—she could now share the burden of the events of the day with him.

Jake said as he gathered her into his arms, "My poor Kathleen, such a day you've had. But don't you feel better now that Billy is in custody?"

"I do," she answered, "but will they keep him?"

"I'll call the police station and try to find out," Jake offered.

He made the call and was told that Billy was being held without bail and with a hearing set for the next week.

Kathleen breathed a sigh of relief. She immediately told the girls and they all felt a lot safer.

The following day Kathleen received two important phone calls. The first was from the mother of the child who had died. She thanked Kathleen in a small, shaken voice for calling the ambulance and staying with Carey until they arrived. She also thanked her for coming forward with the identity of the hit-and-run driver, knowing that eased the pain somewhat. Another call was from the District Attorney's office explaining Kathleen's role as the eyewitness to the accident.

*　　*　　*

The day of the hearing dawned dark and rainy. Kathleen was required to go to the hearing and identify Billy as the hit-and-run driver. Luckily Jake was able to go with her. The prospect of facing Billy again terrified her.

On the way there, Jake admonished her saying, "Calm down, Kathleen. You're fidgeting and jumping around like crazy. Nothing can happen. You'll be perfectly safe."

They entered the courtroom and Kathleen's eyes scanned the room for Billy. She found him quickly, his back to her. As if sensing her presence, he turned slowly around. The look that he gave her was one she would never forget. The evil and hate seemed to challenge her. She began to tremble, but Jake's reassuring closeness calmed her. The hearing proceeded, and at its conclusion, the trial was set for July 9th—two months away.

Kathleen continued to fret, worrying Billy would some-how carry out his threat.

"Kathleen, Billy will be convicted. I really don't know what you are worrying about."

"But," Kathleen replied, "what if he gets paroled? He'll find us and carry out his threats. I know he will."

"Why would he be paroled? I'm sure he'll receive a hefty sentence. You have to stop letting this ruin your life."

Jake was right. They were safe now, and after the trial, Billy would be put away for a long time. But the whole affair had caused Kathleen to become tense, suspicious, and wary. She decided to step up her plans to move as she felt this would make her feel safer. She had been looking for a smaller home to be closer to her job, anyway. The girls hadn't wanted to move, but after the accident, they now agreed.

Chapter Eight

Kathleen opened her eyes. She felt hot and sticky. She wished she had turned the air conditioning on the night before. Suddenly she remembered what today was—July 9th—the day of the trial. She immediately felt nervous and weak.

She forced herself to get up, shower, and dress in a gray suit. When she came downstairs, Jamie and Melissa had breakfast waiting for her.

"Girls, what a surprise! How nice of you."

"Well, Mom, we know this is a big day for you and you need your strength," Melissa said, sounding very grown up.

"I love you girls," Kathleen said as she hugged them to her.

"Billy will be found guilty, won't he, Mom?" Jamie asked.

"I'm almost certain he'll be judged guilty. It's his sentence I'm concerned about," said Kathleen. "You do understand why I don't want you at the trial, don't you?"

"Yes," Melissa replied. "You don't want Billy to see us."

"Right."

The doorbell rang. "That must be Jake," Kathleen said as she walked over and opened the door.

"Hi, girls. Ready, Kathleen? I'm running a tad bit late."

"Oh, I'm ready all right," Kathleen replied nervously. She turned to give both girls a hug. "I'll call you two as soon as we know anything. Marlene will be here any minute to keep you company. Okay?"

"Okay, Mom," Melissa replied. "Good luck."

Kathleen and Jake drove the three miles to the courthouse in silence with Jake's hand resting reassuringly on Kathleen's knee.

As she waited to be called to testify, Kathleen suddenly became very calm. She had nothing to fear from Billy. The judicial system would not fail them. She couldn't continue to live in a terrified state. She had to start trusting.

She walked into the courtroom, again looking for Billy. This time he didn't seem to notice her—no evil stare, no stare at all. He was dressed in a dark brown suit, his white hair limp around his face. She also noticed Carey's parents. They looked tearful and somber but still had a look of anticipation on their faces.

Billy, of course, pleaded not guilty, but with Kathleen's testimony along with evidence found on his car, the jury quickly turned in a guilty verdict. The judge explained that based on Billy's previous record, he was sentencing him to life without parole. Billy continued to look unfocused with no discernible emotion in his pale eyes.

A collective sigh was heard throughout the courtroom. *It seems,* thought Kathleen, *whenever a child is involved, emotions run high.*

Jake hugged Kathleen. "Your ordeal is finally over. Billy is now gone out of your life forever. Let's go to your house, get the girls, and go out and celebrate."

"Okay," Kathleen said, brightening. "That's a great idea."

*   *   *

With Billy in jail, Kathleen found herself thinking about him and the whole terrifying affair less and less. She bought that new house, and she and the girls were busy settling in.

The house was a small, cozy bungalow, with just enough property around it to afford some privacy. Kathleen had told both Jamie and Melissa that they could have a free hand in decorating their rooms. This, of course, delighted them. Kathleen planned to enjoy tending the pretty flower gardens that ran along the front and sides of the house. Jake was a big help with the actual move and in picking out their new puppy—a black Labrador retriever they named Maggie.

*   *   *

Then the impossible happened. It was a beautiful day—unseasonably warm for October. Kathleen was cleaning up around the house and backyard. The girls were off with their friends. As she came into the den from the backyard, she heard the sliding glass doors close behind her. She jumped around expecting to see a child and came face to face with Billy. An involuntary scream came from deep in her throat.

"How can it be? How can you be here? How did you find us?" Kathleen stammered. "Why are you here? What do you want?"

The familiar look of evil was back in his eyes. "Don't worry, I ain't gonna kill you for turning me in. I need you now. You shoulda seen my escape—perfection. And I got a new ID and a place to stay. The only thing is bucks, and I plan to get a steady supply of that from you."

"They'll be looking for you—they'll catch you," Kathleen nearly shouted as terror gripped her.

"With my new ID, and I'm gonna get new hair color and glasses, they'll never get me. And with your money, I'll be just fine."

"I'll go to the police as soon as you leave. I'll tell them you were here."

"Nah, you won't do that," Billy said with a huge smirk on his face, "because if you do, all three of you will be history. You won't know when, but for the rest of your life, you'll be looking over your shoulder for me. Or I can get you killed from inside. I got connections—they owe me and would be real happy to help me out. So, go ahead—call the police."

"Why are you doing this to us?" Kathleen implored near hysterics. "I had to tell the police you hit the child. What else could I do? She died. I'm a mother. I knew how her mother would feel."

"Who cares?" Billy replied with a shrug of indifference. "You'll help me—you got no choice. You'll be hearin' from me every week, where and when will be a big mystery till the time comes. Tell them kids, also, not to tell no one."

Kathleen felt helpless and uncertain as to what to do. Her terror was being replaced by anger. How dare he try to have such control over her? She'd think of a way out—she had to.

Billy finally left, saying he'd contact her soon with the details and demanded she tell him if the police contacted her.

Kathleen dropped to a chair—totally drained and immobilized. How had he escaped? How had he found them? These questions tumbled around inside her head, while the old fears resurfaced. Again she had to tell someone. She knew Jake would go right to the police. Maureen was really the only one she could confide in who would totally abide by her wishes.

She placed the call immediately. Luckily Maureen answered.

"Maureen, he's back. He escaped from jail," Kathleen said, starting to panic again.

"Who? Who's back? Oh, no. Is it Billy? It can't be Billy!"

"Yes, he was just here. He appeared out of no-where—said he escaped. He has a new identity and demands that I give him money. If I don't, and/or tell the police, he said he'll kill the girls and me or have us killed if he's back in prison. What do I do?"

"Oh, man. Let me think. Try to stay calm—I'll call you right back."

How could she stay calm? Kathleen envisioned a lifetime of Billy and nearly broke down.

The next few days were a nightmare. She and Maureen discussed her dilemma thoroughly and could not think of a solution. Kathleen didn't want the girls to know and hoped they wouldn't be home when Billy finally called. Not knowing when he would call was making her frantic.

The police called to let her know about Billy's escape. They felt she was relatively safe because she had moved, but they said they would have a patrol car check her house regularly and for her to report if he did contact her. Kathleen longed to tell them about her encounter with Billy but was too afraid. Those fears—she thought she had conquered them by learning to trust, but she was all confused.

Chapter Nine

Six days later Billy called. Kathleen was to have five hundred dollars ready for him each week. The first payment was due the next day by 11:00 A.M. It was to be delivered, in cash, to a post office box in a neighboring town. She would find a key for it in her mailbox before tomorrow.

After hanging up, Kathleen just stared at the phone. How long could she supply Billy with two thousand dollars a month? She had a considerable amount of savings, but it was not inexhaustible. What would Billy do if she ran out or what if he increased the weekly amount?

The next morning Kathleen found the key in her mailbox. She told the girls she had to run errands and drove over to the post office in Newgate. She placed the five hundred dollars she'd withdrawn from her bank into the designated post office box. She felt a great weight settle over her body, a crushing, trapped feeling. She knew that she had to tell Jake.

"Jake," Kathleen blurted out that night over dinner at his house. "Billy has escaped from prison. He has a new identity and demands that I pay him five hundred dollars a week. He says he'll kill the girls and me if I tell the police. If he's captured because I told the police, he'll arrange to have it done from prison."

Jake jumped up, his face red with anger. "Kathleen, I can't believe you didn't tell me, and the police, as soon as Billy contacted you. You must tell them right away—you're in a very dangerous situation. After he's returned to jail, I'm sure you can enter some kind of a witness protection program and be entirely safe."

Kathleen started to cry. She felt drained and relieved all at once. She should have told Jake right away, should have trusted him. He was right; she had to tell the police.

"Let's call them right now," Kathleen said. "I have the detective's card here in my purse. He even gave me his home number."

They placed the call, and Detective Sullivan said he'd call them at Kathleen's home in one hour. They hurried to her place and arrived just as the phone was ringing. Jake grabbed it up.

"Hello, this is Detective Sullivan. I think we should talk on the phone, as we can't be certain if Billy is or isn't watching Kathleen's movements."

After telling the detective about Billy's plan for a new hair color and glasses plus where the post office box, with number, was located, Detective Sullivan said he didn't think there would be any trouble in apprehending Billy. He asked to speak to Kathleen.

"Yes, Detective? What can I do? As you can imagine, I'm terrified," Kathleen said as she started to tremble.

"We'll have to wait until you hear from Billy again as to when you should drop off the next five hundred dollars. We'll keep patrolling your house as usual, so he doesn't suspect anything. After we've apprehended him, we'll establish new identities for you and the children, and relocate you."

"Thank you, Detective," said a very relieved Kathleen. "I'll be so glad that this nightmare will soon be over. The last thing I want is to have to change identities and move again, but it's a small price to pay to have peace of mind again."

"Okay, call me as soon as Billy makes contact."

"I will, and thank you again for everything," Kathleen said.

Kathleen hung up the phone and gave Jake a huge kiss. "And thank you, Jake. What would I do without you? I felt so trapped—as if I'd fallen down a deep well forever."

"I was thinking," Jake responded, "that this would be a good time to ask you to marry me. We could start a new life as a family."

"Oh, yes. Yes, I will. I love you," Kathleen said, hugging him. "And there is one thing I have finally learned from all this. I will never run from or hide my fears again. I think with your help and love I can do it."

*　　*　　*

It took five days before Billy called again.

"Get the dough there by eleven on Friday morning," he snapped, and then dial tone.

Kathleen told Detective Sullivan, and he said they would start their surveillance early that morning.

Both Kathleen and Jake were very nervous waiting for Friday. They half-expected Billy to call back saying he knew all about the set-up. They jumped every time the phone rang, but he never called back.

On Friday they waited together for word that Billy had been apprehended. It was a long day. By 9:00 P.M. there still was no word. Finally at 11:00 P.M. Detective Sullivan called with news that Billy had been killed. He had had a gun, there was an exchange of fire and Billy died.

"Oh, Jake," Kathleen cried. "It's over, really over. And we don't have to move or change our names."

"Well," Jake said, "I think you will still be changing your name—last one at least."

They both grinned and turned out the light.

Part Three

ALEX

Chapter Ten

Alex slowly opened her green eyes and reached over to caress Nick. When her hand discovered empty space, she remembered she was in San Francisco on a lay-over and heading back to New York today. After fourteen years of working as a flight attendant, she still felt disoriented waking up in a bed different from her own.

Alex smiled as she thought of Nick. He had been the love of her life since she was twenty-two. She remembered clearly the day they had met. She was standing in line at the hardware store near her apartment on East Fifty-third Street. She had changed her mind about her purchase and spun around so quickly that she nearly fell into the arms of the man behind her. After apologizing, she briefly noted that she showed taste into whose arms she fell. The man was ruggedly handsome. He was tall with blonde hair, hazel eyes, a mustache, which was a slightly darker blonde, and a dimple in each cheek. He replied that it was quite all right and promptly asked Alex to have a cup of coffee with him. She accepted, *and the rest,* Alex thought fondly, *was history.*

The phone rang, bringing Alex back to the present.

"Hello?"

"Good morning, this is the operator. It's 6:00 A.M."

"Thanks," Alex said as she hung up, surprised that she hadn't even needed the call.

Alex disliked the early hour, but an early flight meant she'd be back in their apartment right when Nick came home from work. The advertising business kept Nick out late many nights, but tonight they had planned on a nice dinner at their favorite restaurant. Alex wanted everything to be perfect because she was going to bring up the subject of adoption again.

Alex stretched and got up to take a shower. She stopped at the sink and gazed at her reflection in the mirror. Not too bad for thirty-five, she thought. And since she had avoided the party last night, she looked rested. Her blonde hair had gotten too long—time for a trim. What with Alex's pert nose and sensually full lips, Nick always told her how beautiful she was. She thought she was just pretty. She was proud, though, that she had managed to keep her figure trim. She showered, put on her blue uniform, and went down to breakfast.

"Hi, Alex. You missed a good party last night," said her fellow flight attendant, Josie.

"Yeah, good party but not worth the headache I have," replied their purser, Jeff.

"You guys, you'll pay today. Besides, I want to be fresh for my hubby tonight," Alex said. "What time is our pickup?"

"At 7:15—we better get out to the lobby," Josie said. "And where are the others? The captain always has breakfast."

"They must have come down earlier. Let's get going," Jeff said.

On the way to the airport, Alex relaxed in the comfortable silence. She had flown with this crew on the New York to San Francisco line for quite a while. They had become good friends and worked well together. Nearly everyone was married or involved with someone, so they could sidestep the romantic intrigue that went on with many crews. And

Alex was a somewhat shy person, so she enjoyed working with people she knew.

"I hope we're not packed today. Remember last week?" Linda asked.

"Sure do. I don't think we sat down once the entire trip," Jeff replied.

"Just so long as they're pleasant. That's all I ask for," Alex said.

"Amen," Teddy said.

They arrived at the airport and reported to their pre-flight briefing. The flight was nearly full with no celebs or VIPs on board, and there was no bad weather expected. So far, January had been an unusually mild month all over the country.

*   *   *

Captain Wheeler announced the impending touchdown of their flight, American Airlines 186, into New York's LaGuardia Airport. "Flight attendants, please prepare for arrival."

Alex was glad to be back. She liked her job but was always happy to come home. Home to Nick, their seal point Siamese cat, Buttons, and their apartment.

When Alex met Nick, he was living on East Fifty-sixth Street in Manhattan—not far from her own place on East Fifty-third. Since each apartment was small, they found a larger two-bedroom accommodation after they were married.

They had found their garden apartment while reading the Sunday *Times*. It was located on Second Avenue near Eighty-third Street. The building was small and had an elevator. It had a pleasant lobby by New York standards. The apartment had two bedrooms, living room with a dining area, and a walk-through kitchen. Double doors opened into a private hide-a-way garden. That was the clincher. It had stone-terraced sides with small shrubs and flowers and a glorious patch of green grass right in the middle. They took the apartment.

The rent was on the high side, but Nick, at thirty, was doing well in his position at McMannis Advertising Agency. Alex had only been working for the airlines for three years when they were married, but her income helped as well.

Both Alex and Nick liked modern decor. They painted all the walls a sparkling white and added white couches, chrome and glass tables, and colorful area rugs.

*　　*　　*

Alex put her key in the door and pushed the door open with her right shoulder. She was rewarded with the familiar smells of home. Buttons came to her immediately and rubbed her tan-and-white body against Alex's legs, purring loudly.

"Hi, girl. Where's Nick? Not home yet?"

"Who says I'm not home? Come here, you cute stew," Nick said as he engulfed Alex in a bear hug.

"Now how many times do I have to tell you I'm a flight attendant not a stewardess. After eleven years of marriage, I still have to remind you," Alex said, laughing and hugging Nick back.

"Okay, okay—you win—Miss flight attendant. How was your day? Busy flight?"

"It was pretty full, and we were on our feet most of the flight, but no major problems. I think I'll soak in a hot tub before we go out. Want to join me?" Alex asked.

"I would, but you go ahead. I have a few phone calls to make. I'll bring you in a nice glass of wine."

"Mmmmmmm . . . sounds perfect."

*   *   *

Sitting at Trotti's after dinner, Alex swallowed hard and said, "Nick, we've had every test and even tried artificial insemination and in vitro fertilization with no success. I think it's time we talk seriously about adoption."

Silence hung heavy between them.

Finally Nick said, "You know I'm not real excited about that idea. I just can't imagine why you don't get pregnant. Every doctor we've seen says there's nothing wrong with either of us. You know I want a child as much as you do. It's so frustrating."

Alex found herself starting to cry. She hated to cry, but Nick was right. They had endured five frustrating years trying to conceive. If only love were enough, they'd have five children by now.

Nick took Alex's hand. "Oh, sweetheart, please don't cry. You're too beautiful to be sad. I guess there'd be no harm in at least going to talk to an adoption agency."

Alex brightened and smiled through her tears. "I love you, Nick. I love you so much. Are you sure?"

"I don't promise anything, but I'll keep an open mind."

*   *   *

Alex began their search armed with the phone book and several newspapers. They had no family or close friends who had ever adopted, so they were pretty much on their own to dig up information and explore possibilities.

After several days of phone calls, Alex found two agencies that she liked. One dealt with domestic adoptions and the other international.

Alex reported to Nick what she had discovered. "I found one domestic agency that sounded very caring and helpful. It takes them roughly twelve months to find a newborn,

Caucasian infant. The others I called take longer. I made an initial appointment with the one agency week after next."

"Sounds good. Anything else?" Nick asked.

"I also located an agency that places foreign children from South America and Korea. The children are older when adopted, three to six months, but the placement wait is typically only six months. Oh, and also you must travel to the country to pick up the child. Sounds interesting, don't you think?"

"Would we really want to get involved with that? I think we're better off sticking with our own country. Wouldn't that be better?" Nick asked, looking anxious.

"I just want a baby to love, for us to love together. But if you're more comfortable with an American infant, I can wait the possible year," Alex said, as she searched Nick's face waiting for his response.

Nick looked relieved, his features softened and relaxed. "Why don't we talk with the domestic agency and go from there?"

Alex wrapped her arms around Nick's neck and kissed him softly. "Okay."

Chapter Eleven

Winter had made a comeback. Alex shivered as she listened to the radio's forecast predicting wind chills at twenty degrees below zero.

Looking out the window at the steel-gray overcast sky and barren trees in the park across from their apartment, Alex thought things dull and drab. She wouldn't, however, let anything ruin the anticipation and excitement she felt for their appointment with the Family Resource Adoption Agency at 2:00 P.M.

Alex dressed in a red, black, and white knit dress. She secured her blonde hair back with a red bow. She wanted to appear respectable and capable but not dull.

"How do I look?" asked Nick, coming into view at Alex's mirror. "Do I look trustworthy or sinister?"

Alex thought he looked very handsome in a navy suit, white striped shirt, and classy silk tie. "Definitely trustworthy. How about me?"

"You, my dear, look every bit the potential mommy. Oh, and also PTA chairman and Brownie troop leader."

Alex smiled. "Then I guess we're ready. Let's go see what they have to say."

They took a cab to an office building on Forty-third and Madison. On the way up in the elevator, Nick reached for Alex's hand and gave her a long, measuring look.

"You look nervous. Are you nervous?"

"I'm mostly excited, but also a wee bit nervous," Alex admitted.

"Just remember this is only a start. I'm sure there are other options to explore," Nick said.

Alex gave Nick's arm a squeeze and was thinking about how heartened she was by Nick's warming to the idea of adoption, when the elevator door opened into a large room with comfortable-looking couches and chairs. There were quite a few photos of children on the walls. It looked so non-threatening that Alex found herself relaxing some. An attractive brunette with a broad, open face who looked to be about fifty walked out of a side door.

"So nice to meet you, Mr. and Mrs. Stone," she said extending a hand. "I'm Janet Abrahms. Sit down, please."

Janet Abrahms proceeded to give Alex and Nick an overview of the agency and services offered. She explained the probable time frame for adoption and the fees.

"Here's an application for you to fill out at your leisure and return to us. Then we'll set up an in-depth conference for you with one of our counselors."

"Thank you, Ms. Abrahms. You've been very helpful," Nick said, rising.

Nick and Alex left the office with their heads spinning. Janet Abrahms had thrown a lot of material at them.

"Oh, Nick, didn't she say a year to several years?" Alex asked incredulously when they were back in the lobby.

"I think she did, why?"

"Well, when I called them, they said one year. That's why I made an appointment."

"It may take longer than one year, Alex. That's all. I think Ms. Abrahms sounded very encouraging."

"Then forget it! I won't wait that long. I've already waited long enough." Alex's voice was rising. "We'll just have to try the foreign route—only six months. I can't wait any longer, Nick. Do you understand?"

Alex was near hysterics. She had thought this agency would be the answer to their dreams.

Nick gathered Alex into his arms. "I know, sweetie, I know," he murmured into her soft, silky hair.

Alex's shoulders shook as she let loose with a torrent of tears. She didn't care where they were or who heard. She was devastated. She had endured so many tests and procedures. Surely, she had thought, adoption would be easy in comparison.

Nick steered Alex into a coffee shop. "We need to sit down calmly and talk, Alex. Why don't you go into the ladies room and splash some water on your face? You'll feel better."

Alex did as Nick suggested. Bending over the sink, she peered into the mirror. Her usually pretty face was pinched and puffy. Nick was right. She had to get a grip. This was just the start. How could she have thought that this very first interview would magically produce a baby for them? She would have to be more patient even though everything inside her screamed how unfair it was.

*   *   *

Between Alex's flights and Nick's busy work schedule, they talked with three more agencies—one of which placed foreign babies. Nick tried to keep an open mind but finally told Alex he couldn't do it. He wanted an American child. Alex understood but was terribly disappointed.

One night at the beginning of March, Nick came home with promising news. "Alex, an acquaintance at work today told me of a lawyer who arranges private adoptions. His sister and her husband adopted a beautiful baby girl through this guy."

Alex's eyes opened wide. "Why didn't we ever think of that? Do you have his name? Is he here in New York? Can he find us a baby right away?" The questions tumbled out.

"Yes to all but the time factor. There are no guarantees, but he found the sister's baby in eight months."

Alex became very excited. Then, she immediately drew back. Was it too good to be true? Was there a catch?

"Is there anything you're not telling me? Is it legal, Nick?"

"I did a little checking and it's absolutely above board and legal. The only drawback is the expense—it's very expensive."

"Too expensive?" Alex asked hesitantly.

"We'll manage. We want our son, don't we?"

Alex flew into Nick's arms, smothering him with kisses. "Really? We can contact the lawyer?"

"Yes, we can contact the lawyer. You have me as involved in this as you are!"

"Heh, wait a minute," Alex said, smiling. "What was that about a son? No daughter?"

"Just a slip, I guess. Either a son or a daughter would be just fine. How's that?"

"Exactly what I was hoping to hear."

*   *   *

Alex sat at their kitchen table enjoying a ray of sunshine as it played across her face. Even though spring had officially started two days before, they were still very much in winter's grip. Alex allowed herself to think of all the things she had to be thankful for. First there was Nick. She loved him as much now as she did the day they were married. She had heard of passion and love diminishing over time, but this was not the case with her. She also enjoyed her job and adored their apartment. The only thing missing was a child. But now that they had contacted the attorney, Lawrence Bennett, Alex was hopeful a baby would soon be theirs.

One week earlier Alex and Nick had met with Mr. Bennett. He was an outgoing, friendly sort of man who looked to be in his forties. He explained that many of his family were attorneys, but that the criminal law practices they had did not interest him. Instead, he derived satisfaction from helping unwanted or unplanned for babies find loving homes.

After talking together for several hours, both Alex and Nick and Mr. Bennett felt comfortable enough to proceed. Papers were signed, fees agreed to, and Alex and Nick had nothing left to do but wait.

Just knowing they had taken a concrete step towards finding a child allowed Alex and Nick to relax a bit. Any tension that had been building between them seemed to abate. They took pleasure once again in everyday things and even planned to drive out to the Hamptons to their favorite bed-and-breakfast once the weather warmed.

*   *   *

It was the first weekend in June before either Alex or Nick could get away for a weekend. May had been cool anyway, so they didn't mind waiting.

"Oh, what a gorgeous day," Alex declared as they drove in their white Nissan along the Long Island Expressway. The windows were down, and she let the breeze ruffle her hair. Everything was so green and fresh. "I'll actually be glad to get away from the phone for a few days. I find myself willing it to ring with word from Mr. Bennett whenever I'm in the apartment. It's exhausting. I know we must be patient, but it has been almost three months and we haven't heard a thing yet."

"He said he'd call us as soon as he had a lead," Nick replied. "Give it some more time. I know it's hard to wait, but I have a good feeling about this. Let's enjoy the summer, knowing that a surprise could happen at anytime."

A surprise. What a wonderful way to think about the wait, Alex thought. The wait for a baby to make them a family.

Chapter Twelve

The alarm went off. Nick moaned and rolled over to kiss Alex. "It's not fair that you can sleep and I have to get up and trudge to work."

"Hey, you. I just got back from a flight. I did my time for a while. Man, is it cold in here. Would you please turn down the air conditioner? And have a nice day, sweetheart."

"You, too. I'll call you later," Nick said as he gave Alex a kiss on the tip of her nose.

Alex awoke again at 8:30. She stretched, noticing what a bright sunny day it was. She smiled to herself and pledged not to even think about the phone today. After all, it was only July—four months since they had talked with Mr. Bennett.

No, today was a gift from above. Alex planned to garden in their lovely little backyard and then leisurely relax in the sun—reading that new novel she had picked up at the airport.

As she stepped out into the garden to enjoy her breakfast, Alex was once again aware of the beauty of the day. Her flowers, planted with loving care one month ago, were blooming in vivid colors of pink, white, purple, and yellow. The sky was a deep blue without a cloud in sight. Everything seemed sharp and clear, almost intense in its perfection.

Before eating, Alex proceeded to do that which she never tired of doing—walk barefoot through their little patch of genuine green grass. She delighted in the surprisingly soft caress of the blades on the soles of her feet. She was interrupted by the ringing of the phone.

As usual, Alex felt her stomach lurch at the sound but instantly reminded herself of her resolve. It was probably Nick anyway. She reached for the phone.

"Hello?"

"Well, hello there. Is this Mrs. Stone?"

"Yes," Alex replied tentatively.

"This is Lawrence Bennett. I know it's been a while, but I've been tied up finding the young lady in Texas who will be giving birth to your baby three months from now."

Alex started to tremble. Could it really be? Was she imagining this? Tears ran down her cheeks unnoticed.

With a hoarse voice, Alex asked, "Really, truly, you found us a baby? A real live baby!"

"Why, of course it's a real live baby." Bennett chuckled. "Listen, I know you want to call your husband with the good news. Why don't you both come on down to my office tomorrow, and I'll have all the details for you. How about 11:00 A.M.?"

Alex found her voice again. "Oh, yes. We'll be there, Mr. Bennett. And thank you, thank you so much."

Alex immediately called Nick. "Nick, we have our baby!" she nearly screamed into the phone.

"What? Bennett called? Oh, shit—I can't believe it. Yes, I can. I told you a surprise would be coming our way. What did Bennett tell you?"

"He just said that the young girl was in Texas and was due to deliver in three months," Alex said excitedly. "And to come to his office tomorrow at 11:00 A.M."

"We'll be there. I love you, Alex. I know we've waited a long time for this."

"And I love you too, Daddy. Hurry home."

"Pinch me," Alex asked. "Are we really going to be parents soon?"

"We are. We'll have our baby in three months. Three short months." Nick smiled.

"Charlene has definitely made the right decision. Don't you think?" Alex asked. "I mean, seventeen is much too young to take care of a baby. She's only in high school. She's a child herself."

"I think she did make the right decision, but it must have been confusing and hard for her," Nick replied. "Must still be."

Lawrence Bennett had all the papers ready for them to sign when Alex and Nick had gone to his office. He explained that Charlene Morgan was an unmarried teenager from Dallas, Texas. Her parents convinced her that adoption was the only option available to her, and neither parents nor Charlene had any desire to meet Alex and Nick. The baby was due on October 25th. One week after the birth, the baby was to be theirs. They would travel to Dallas at that time to pick up their newborn.

*   *   *

The rest of the summer was planned around setting up the baby's nursery, with a few pleasure trips out to the Hamptons.

On one such trip, tragedy struck. Nick, at the wheel of their Nissan, was easing out into the expressway. Without any warning whatsoever, they were hit broadside by another car.

The last thing Alex remembered was the terror she saw in Nick's eyes before her head hit the windshield.

Chapter Thirteen

Alex had suffered a skull fracture in the accident. She had been in a coma for two weeks. Nick's broken leg and arm were troublesome, but he hardly noticed as he sat quietly by Alex's bed night and day. Nurses insisted he grab some sleep each night, but otherwise he was by Alex's side—waiting for her to awake. He talked to her endlessly about the baby. She just had to get well because the baby was coming soon.

"Why doesn't she wake up?" Nick asked Alex's doctor. "You said the fracture was stable and mending. When will she wake up?"

"These things are always unpredictable, Nick. It may be soon or it may take a while longer."

"But what if she never wakes up?" Nick asked, with panic in his voice.

"We believe she will. All her tests are positive. There's no choice but to wait. I'm sorry," the doctor said.

Wait. Wait. Nick could no longer stand the word. Wait for a baby, wait for Alex to wake up. He felt as though he might scream.

Two days later Alex did open her eyes. She blinked, trying to remember what had happened to her. She instinctively knew something was wrong, but she couldn't place what it was. She focused on a man's face. She knew that face, it would come to her.

"Oh, Alex, my dear sweet Alex." The man was kissing

her face all over. She could taste his salty tears. The anguish in his eyes was puzzling.

"Alex, it's me Nick," Nick said into her questioning eyes.

A nurse came in with the doctor, and Nick was asked to leave. Fifteen minutes later Dr. Moran came out of Alex's room.

"What's wrong with her, Doctor? Why doesn't she recognize me?" Nick asked frantically.

"She appears to be suffering from amnesia—loss of memory. Why don't you get some sleep and in the morning we'll run a few more tests. She's asleep and will remain so for the remainder of the night, so please go home."

Nick was stunned. How could Alex not know him? What if she never regained her memory? And the baby. What about the baby? He wept unashamedly.

"It appears," Dr. Moran told Nick the next day, "that your wife is suffering from amnesia, but our tests show no permanent damage. It may be, however, that she will have to relearn many things."

"What things?" Nick asked.

"Well, most likely you will have to reacquaint her with your shared relationship. She may even have to learn the basics of eating, talking, and walking again."

*   *   *

"Nick," Alex called. "I'm tired of these exercises. When can I go home?"

"I told you, sweetheart, we all want to make sure you are well before you do go home."

Alex had been at the Rehabilitation Institute of Long Island for two months. In that time, she had gradually recalled Nick and their life together. And she had worked very hard to learn to be the person she once was.

"Tell me again what the lawyer told you about Charlene's pregnancy," Alex asked.

"Well, she's due in one month. Everything is going well. Both mother and child are healthy. Depending on your strength, we'll go down to get her one week after she's born as planned. Bennett will notify us the minute the baby is born with details of its health, sex, and weight."

"Oh, Nick, I can feel her and smell her already. She's helping me get better. She wants me to be her mommy," Alex said, blinking back tears.

"What if she's a he? Remember we talked about that. And what about me? I thought I was kind of important in your recovery."

Alex drew him close. "You are. I love you so. I truly couldn't have done it without you either. And a he is fine also, you know that."

*   *   *

They got the call in the apartment at 1:00 A.M. on Friday, October 26.

Bennett's voice sounded as proud as a grandpa's. "Charlene just delivered a healthy, nine-pound baby girl. Congratulations."

Nick dropped the phone and turned to Alex. "It's a girl, a little girl."

"A girl. I knew it was going to be a girl. Our daughter!" exclaimed Alex through a mixture of tears and smiles.

Alex and Nick hugged and smiled and laughed—feeling drunk with joy.

"Hello, hello."

Nick heard the voice and remembered Bennett was still on the phone.

"Sorry," Nick said, picking up the receiver. "So what happens next?"

"We'll fly down next weekend to Dallas. Everything should be in order by then. Will Mrs. Stone be able to make the trip?"

"You bet. She's made a complete recovery."

"Okay then, until next week. Congratulations again to you both."

"Thank you, Mr. Bennett. Thank you so very much."

*　　*　　*

Erika Jane Stone, at five weeks, had her parents completely wrapped around her little finger. They didn't mind though. They couldn't do enough for her. Even as they ran circles around her, they reminded themselves that they must not spoil her.

"Just look at her, Nick," Alex marveled. "Ten perfect little toes and ten perfect little fingers. Do you think she'll ever get any hair? And do you think her eyes will stay blue?"

Nick hugged them both as Alex cradled Erika in her arms. "I don't know, but won't we have fun watching her over the years to find out."

Alex and Nick exchanged a smile. A smile that said their family was finally complete.

Epilogue

Looking down at Erika's sweet, slumbering face, Alex was overwhelmed by feelings of gratitude and love. Her gratitude reached across the miles to Charlene, Erika's birth mother. She felt sadness for this young girl whose arms would never encircle this precious child.

Alex suddenly felt an urge to find her own birth mother. She'd never been curious before, not before Erika. She wondered where her mother lived. Did she have any regrets of giving Alex up for adoption? Alex also wondered if she had any siblings. More than once, as she was growing up, Alex had experienced a feeling—a feeling that she had a kindred spirit out there somewhere.

Perhaps tomorrow she would make a few phone calls.